THE Truth About UNICORNS

by Tracy Sue Walker

illustrated by Chris Jevons

SCHOLASTIC INC.

ISBN 978-1-338-54739-9

10 9 8 7 6 5 4 3 2   19 20 21 22 23

Printed in the U.S.A.   40
First printing 2019

Book design by Jennifer Rinaldi

CHAPTER ONE
JOIN THE CLUB

OKAY, YOU HAVE TO PICK—HORSES OR UNICORNS? Hard choice, but I bet you went with the one-horned wonders, didn't you? You're not alone. It's hard to resist creatures that poop rainbows, unless you know what they're really like. That's how The Kids for Truth about Magical Creatures started. KTMC for short. I'm Julian Fillmore, by the way, and my friends Ava and Sarah and I aren't fooled. We know Magical Creatures aren't all moonbeams and jazz hands. And we're going to prove it. Don't believe me? I have three words for you. Sugar. The. Unicorn.

I look at my watch. It's 4:20 p.m. We were supposed to start at 4 o'clock.

I turn to Sarah and Ava and shrug my shoulders. "Well?"

"Give it five more minutes," Sarah says as she

draws a circle in the dirt with the toe of her shoe.

Ava rolls her eyes. "That's what you said five minutes ago."

We're sitting on our school playground benches because that's where we can fit the most people. Ava has a cake pan covered with aluminum foil on her lap, and she keeps pinching the edges around the corners.

"Look, if no one shows up for a meeting when we have free cupcakes and cheese puffs," Ava says, "they're not showing up. Ever."

Sarah gives me a sideways glance when I slide my hand out of the cheese puff bag and pop one in my mouth. "Those are for our new members," she says.

"Sorry," I say as little flecks of cheese dust dribble down my navy blue shirt.

"I can't believe no one came," Sarah says, slumping her shoulders. She tosses a piece of gravel, and it pings off one of the metal swing set poles.

This is our third meeting of The Kids for Truth about Magical Creatures, and we're still the only three members.

"I can believe it," I say. "Everybody voted for our classroom to have a Magical Creatures theme this year except us."

Sarah ignores me and turns to Ava. "Did you hand out the flyers?"

Ava reaches into her backpack and pulls out a sheet of paper with a red, white, and blue wavy border.

Join The

KIDS FOR TRUTH ABOUT MAGICAL CREATURES!!!

Think baboons are more interesting than Big Foot?

Dogs are better than Dragons?

Are you fed up with Magicals hogging the spotlight?

Think Ordinaries deserve some respect?

JOIN THE KTMC!

Meeting Today at the Playground Benches

4 p.m. • FREE SNACKS!!!!!

"I stuck one in every locker at lunchtime," Ava says, looking peeved. "A lot of good *that* did!"

She peels back the aluminum foil on her cake pan, and there are four perfect rows of strawberry cupcakes. Each cupcake has a little sign on a toothpick sticking out of it. She hands me one. Mine says, ORDINARY CREATURES ARE BERRY NICE!

"Start the meeting," Ava says as she licks strawberry icing off her thumb. "We're busy people. We all have lives."

I clear my throat and stand facing the bench. "I call to order the third meeting of The Kids for Truth about Magical Creatures!"

"You don't have to shout," Ava says. "All two of us can hear you."

Sarah starts writing in the notebook she has balanced on her lap. She volunteered to be our club secretary, which means she keeps track of what we talk about and types it up so we don't forget.

"Did everybody bring their pick of which Magical Creature we should investigate first?" I ask, but before Ava and Sarah can answer, Brandon

Henderson's mom pulls into the parking lot in a white pickup truck, towing their Magical Utility Vehicle. The MUV has a speaker mounted on its roof, and whenever it's in motion, it plays twinkly little tunes like an ice cream truck. "Do Your Ears Hang Low?" is drifting our way.

Brandon is in our class and was a big supporter of the whole Magical Creatures theme for our classroom. He was also one of my best friends until Sugar arrived. When Mrs. Henderson parks, the music stops. She gets out and walks toward us.

"Hi, kids!" she waves. Sarah and I sort of wave, but Ava doesn't let go of her cupcakes.

"Brandon has strep throat," she says, and wood chips crunch under her feet as she walks past the slide on her way to the benches. "Mrs. Frisner is giving me his homework."

Just like me, Ava, and Sarah, Brandon is one of Frisner's Prisoners. That's what the rest of the school calls us. It sounds harsh, but hear me out. For one thing, Mrs. Frisner's voice sounds like the engine in my grandma's old minivan; it's loud and rattles a lot.

Then there are the worksheets. If you stretched all of Mrs. Frisner's worksheets end to end, they would circle the earth three times.

But all that's a walk in the park compared to the thing that drove the three of us over the edge—all the Magical Creatures. Bigfoot on the bulletin boards, mermaids on the walls, dragon decals on the windows. Ava got up the nerve to ask Mrs. Frisner if we could decorate with some Ordinary Creatures, too.

"Puppies or kittens?" Ava asked. "Or bunnies? Bunnies are nice."

"I like the Magicals, Miss Chen," Mrs. Frisner said, and then she sighed so hard I thought she injured a lung. "They take me to my happy place. Now, sit down and get back to your worksheet."

That's why the three of us started KTMC.

Mrs. Henderson pats me on the shoulder. "We haven't seen you in a while, Julian. Come by. Please. Brandon would like that."

"Yeah, okay," I say halfheartedly as she turns around and heads toward the school building. Brandon might like it, but Sugar would not.

The MUV looks like a horse trailer only better. Much better. The whole thing is painted in glittery bubble gum pink with purple stars all over, and on its side in turquoise, curlicue letters is the name of Brandon's unicorn—Sugar!! Worst of all, the dots on the exclamation points make a smiley face.

"It looks like a rainbow threw up all over that thing," Ava says. "I'll get my camera."

"Is it on a normal setting?" I joke, and she ignores me.

Ava is always taking photos but not any old kind—macro shots. You know, pictures of stuff so up close you can't tell what it is. It's her passion. So far, we've been treated to extreme close-ups of tree bark, her little brother's pinky toe nail, and the left nostril of Pickles, the zoo's aardvark.

While Ava's snapping shots of Sugar's MUV from a distance, Sarah starts singing under her breath, *"Do your ears hang low? Do they wobble to and fro? Can you tie 'em in a knot? Can you tie 'em in a bow?"*

"Would you stop that?" Ava says, putting her hand on her hip. "I'm trying to concentrate."

"Sorry," Sarah says. "It's stuck in my brain."

"I don't know any ponies or horses that travel like that," Ava says.

"There has to be a reason they get such special treatment," Sarah says, "but what is it?"

"Does it matter?" I ask. "You're way too easy on Magicals, Sarah. That MUV just proves our point; it's not fair Magicals are treated so much better. Ordinaries deserve justice."

"And we're going to prove it," Ava says. She sounds determined. "These photos will be perfect for *Creature Feature*."

Creature Feature is the KTMC blog, and this investigation will be our first post. We figured it was the best way to share our findings and prove our point about Magicals and Ordinaries. I'm our official writer, and it's the first big step toward my dream. Blogger today, star reporter tomorrow.

Ava is about to take another round of photos when we hear the school door open, so she stuffs the camera in her backpack. Mrs. Henderson has one of Mrs. Frisner's red homework folders tucked under her arm. She waves to us and gets back in the pickup truck. "The Farmer in the Dell" blasts from the

speaker when she starts the engine, and bubbles float out of a little pipe on the roof and drift across the parking lot. We stare as the MUV rolls away. The music fades, and we're left with the sound of the swings clinking together on the empty playground.

"Back to business!" Ava says. "And I vote for unicorns, by the way. The bubbles made up my mind."

Sarah nods, "Fine by me; any Magical will be fascinating to investigate. Julian, what say you?"

I nod slowly. Unicorns it is. They're the vainest, most self-centered, obnoxious Magicals there are, especially one unicorn in particular.

Ava passes the pan of cupcakes around, and Sarah picks up her notebook. They both look at me.

"If we want justice for Ordinaries," I say, "and to prove unicorns are just rainbow-colored frauds, then there's one thing we need."

"What's that?" Ava asks, raising her eyebrows.

"A master plan!"

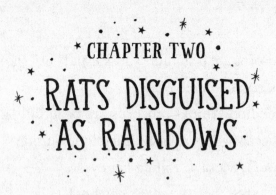

CHAPTER TWO

RATS DISGUISED AS RAINBOWS

"So what's the plan?" Sarah asks.

"We need to build our case!" I say, because that's what they're always yelling about on my mom's favorite show, *Angry Law*. My mom's a lawyer, too, but she's never in a courtroom like the lawyers on the show. She works for a company that makes plastic cafeteria trays, and she makes sure they pay their taxes the right way.

"We need arguments!" I say. That's something else they're always saying on *Angry Law*. "Here's what I think we should do. Everybody come up with one thing about unicorns, something everyone else believes that you want to prove isn't true."

We take a few minutes to think until Ava breaks the silence. "Got one!"

"Let's hear it," I say.

"Unicorns are beautiful—inside and out," she says.

"Yes—good one!" I say.

"Everybody thinks unicorns are beautiful on the inside because they're beautiful on the outside. Total nonsense," Ava says, rolling her eyes.

She takes her science notebook out of her backpack. "Listen to this. Dolphins use echolocation, right?" She looks at me and Sarah like we know what that is. We shrug and Ava sighs. "They make high-pitched noises that bounce off things underwater so they know what and where stuff is. Well, it turns out, unicorns use echolocation, too. But get this, dolphins use it to locate other dolphins, or coral reefs, or boats. Unicorns only use it to locate mirrors. Can you believe that?"

I believe it. Sugar looks like she's never met a mirror she didn't like.

Ava goes on. "So they've developed these super-high-pitched squeals that are too high for human or even dog ears to hear, just so they can find mirrors. My brother's copy of *Amazing Magical Factoids* says they can locate a mirror the size of a quarter from over five miles away."

"Give me a break," Sarah says.

"That's the worst magical superpower ever," I say. "Superman would get his butt kicked all the time if all he could do was locate mirrors."

"For real," Ava says. "All that inner beauty stuff they want you to believe is false advertising. Unicorns are the vainest Magicals out there."

"That's a good start," Sarah says, and turns to me. "Okay, blog master. You're next."

"Well, you know how people are always saying that unicorns make the best friends?" I say, and Sarah and Ava nod. "Well, how can something so self-centered be a great friend? It doesn't make sense. And unicorn owners are just as bad. As soon as they have something shiny and magical, they forget about their non-magical friends.

"And what's with unicorn names?" I go on. "Gumdrop. Cupcake. Sprinkles." I feel my voice getting louder with each stupid name. The tips of my ears are burning, too; they always do that when I'm upset.

"That's my argument," I say firmly. "I'm going to prove that unicorns are not the friendly creatures people think they are. They're rats disguised as rainbows."

"You okay, Julian?" Sarah asks.

"Great," I say, clenching my jaw. "Never better."

"It's getting late," Ava says. "Sarah, you're up next."

Sarah looks at her notes. "Unicorns seem to be scared of *everything*. I read in *Magical Monthly* that they're afraid of rain, getting their hooves dirty, and lightning."

I take a deep breath.

"Julian's afraid of lightning," Ava says.

"I've got my reasons," I say, clenching my jaw

again. If Ava and Sarah think I'm going to tell them why I hate lightning, they're wrong. "So . . . unicorns are cowards," I say to get us back on track.

"Apparently," Sarah says. "But I wonder why? Maybe they've got good reasons, too."

"I doubt it," I say, and look at my watch. It's 5 o'clock, and my dad asked me to help him make dinner. "I have to go."

"So? What comes next?" Sarah asks.

"Evidence," I say. That's another topic on *Angry Law*. They're always collecting evidence. "Everybody do their research. We'll meet back here a week from today and share what we've found."

"I'll be ready," Ava says.

"Me too!" Sarah agrees.

"Me three," I say. "The unicorns won't know what hit 'em!"

CHAPTER THREE
MIRROR, MIRROR

"C'MON, MISTER FILLMORE. DON'T DAWDLE!" IT'S time for our next meeting, and I hear Mrs. Frisner's gravelly voice behind me while I'm getting my evidence together at my locker.

"TODAY, Mister Fillmore. I'd like to leave before my two-hundredth birthday," she says as I zip the pockets on my backpack.

"And that goes for Miss Chen and Miss Marco, too!" she calls after me as I run toward the exit where Ava and Sarah are waiting. Ava tucks a long cardboard tube and a metal folded thing under her arm, and we run out the door before Mrs. Frisner can yell at us again.

"What's all that?" I ask her.

"Evidence," Ava says, and grins.

At the benches, she opens the folded metal object. It's a portable easel. "I borrowed it from my dad," she says. Then she opens the long cardboard tube and pulls out a couple rolls of paper.

Sarah shoots me a look.

"What?" Ava says. "Some of this is easier to explain using charts and graphs."

She unrolls the first paper. "I'd like to present my first piece of evidence against unicorns being beautiful inside and out," she says.

If Ava was wearing a suit instead of a T-shirt that says I TALK TO MYSELF WHEN I NEED EXPERT ADVICE, she'd look like the lawyers on *Angry Law*. She clips a bar graph to the easel. It's titled *Mirror Usage in Unicorn Populated Areas*.

"I went to work with my dad last Saturday," Ava says. Her dad's a professor, and they hang out at

the university library together. "I did a lot of reading," she continues, "and it turns out that mirror sales quadrupled last year in areas that are highly populated with unicorns. That's four times the number of mirrors sold—

solid proof that unicorns are vain."

"You know," Sarah says. "When I was trying to find stuff about whether they're brave or not, I saw an article on *Extra-Ordinaries* that said unicorns don't like giving rides to most people. They're 'highly selective' when it comes to riders."

"Snobs," I say, "with their Magical noses in the air." Ava snorts. She does that when she thinks something is really funny.

She unfurls the second roll and clips a pie chart to the easel.

How Unicorns Spend Their Time

*statistics from The American Journal of the Magical Mind, vol. 45, no. 9, pp29-30

40% — Time spent admiring themselves

30% — Time spent on beauty routines

20% — Time spent being admired by humans

9% — Time spent admiring other unicorns

1% — Time spent trying to think deep thoughts

"Additional proof," she says, using a ruler to point to the four largest slices on the chart. "Ninety-nine percent of a unicorn's time is spent on their outer beauty. Only one percent is spent on inner."

"Can we post that on *Creature Feature*?" I ask Ava.

"Oh yeah! I created it based on statistics I found in a scientific journal at the library."

"All this just proves what I've thought all along based on Brandon," I say.

"What do you mean?" Sarah asks.

This was going to come out eventually. "Brandon's family brought Sugar home about a year ago, and it all made sense at first. You guys know Brandon's dad is a veterinarian, and that's why they got Toby all those years ago. He wanted his son to grow up with a pony."

"I didn't know they had Toby that long," Sarah says.

"Since Brandon was a baby," I say. "Then at Angela Esposito's birthday party last year Brandon met her unicorn, Lollipop. All of a sudden, he wanted to know everything there was to know about unicorns. Tells his dad he wants to be a Magical Creature vet who specializes in—guess what?"

"Unicorns," Ava says.

"That's when Dr. Henderson decided to get Sugar, so Brandon could learn about unicorn behavior, their eating habits. All that stuff."

"What's so bad about that?" Sarah shrugs.

"Nothing," I say, "unless you completely ignore the pony that's been loyal to you your whole life. I watched it happen."

"That's so sad," Sarah says.

"Sad doesn't even begin to cover it," I say. "Now Brandon spends all his free time with that unicorn; time he used to spend with Toby, time he used to spend playing soccer with me. Hey, who needs a best friend when you've got a stupid, self-centered unicorn, right? Now Toby's ignored while Brandon brushes and braids and perfumes Sugar . . ."

"Perfumes?" Ava asks, wrinkling her nose.

"Ever smelled a unicorn?" I ask.

She shakes her head.

"It's . . . unique," I say. "Imagine a combination

of sweaty tennis shoes and sour milk."

"Ewwww," Ava says.

"Exactly," I answer.

"I think we've proven our point about them not being beautiful *inside* just because they're beautiful *outside*," Ava says. "You think we should include photos of Toby and Sugar in *Creature Feature*? It would really demonstrate how Magicals receive special treatment."

"Photos make it personal. Readers will relate to what we're writing about," Sarah nods as she takes a few more notes. "Okay, we've got our first argument, but there's a lot more to understand."

"Absolutely," I say, and while Ava is rolling up her charts and graphs and folding her easel, I stand up with my white, lined notecards in hand.

There is no worse friend in this world than a unicorn. And I've got the evidence to prove it.

CHAPTER FOUR
BEST FRENEMIES

"YOU KNOW THAT AD FOR MAGICAL MART—THE one that says, 'Walk into Magical Mart and walk out with a best friend'? They show that girl going home with a purple-striped unicorn?" I ask.

Ava and Sarah nod.

"Lies!" I say. "All lies. There are so many reasons unicorns are terrible friends, but we don't have all day, so here are a few."

I look down at my notecards. "First, they spend way too much time on beauty. There's no time left for any*thing* or any*one* else."

"Yes!" Ava agrees.

"Do you know any ponies who insist on having their hooves painted or their manes curled on a regular basis?" I ask. "Didn't think so."

I flip to the next card. "Their owners have to drive unicorns to parks and malls because they insist on being admired by the public."

"Truth," Sarah says. "When I'm at the park for my tennis lessons, there's always a herd of them standing by the fountain like statues."

I flip to the next card. "And don't get me started on Sugar's shampoo ads. Since Brandon's mom signed her up with that talent agency, she's gone all the time. Some friend that is."

"That doesn't sound like it's her fault," Sarah says. She sounds way too sympathetic. "If Mrs. Henderson signed her up, she's just going where they take her."

"Oh, I guarantee she has a say," I add. "The first time I met Sugar, she was on her way to Hair and Hooves Parlor to have her mane spruced up for one of those ads. I tried to talk to her. I walked over to meet her; I even brought her some sugar cubes from home. Do you think she was happy to meet me?"

"I'm guessing the answer is no," Ava says.

"She told me she had an important appointment that afternoon and she didn't have time to talk. Fine. I can take a hint. Wait until I write about this on *Creature Feature*."

"I don't think you should put your personal feelings on the blog, Julian," Ava says. "We should stick to the facts; it's more scientific that way."

I ignore her, and my ears are burning again as I flip to the last card. "One more thing! All this stuff about unicorns being great pets—I don't buy it. Have you ever seen a pile of unicorn droppings? There's no way to camouflage a huge, glittery, glowing pile of rainbow poop."

"I'm saying this now so everyone hears," Ava says. "I'm happy to take photos of Toby and Sugar. I'm happy to take photos of an aardvark's nose. But I am *not* taking photos of unicorn poop."

"Duly noted," Sarah says, and jots it down in her notebook.

"So that's my proof that unicorns are lousy

friends," I say. My ears are still burning.

"That's more than enough evidence," Ava says. "They've already got two strikes against them. Sarah's the third."

"Wait," Sarah says. "You haven't heard *my* evidence yet."

"You're not going to tell us unicorns are the bravest Magical Creatures out there, are you?" I can't help laughing when I ask.

"Maybe," Sarah says. "You won't know until you hear my evidence, and here it comes, so hold on to your gym socks!"

CHAPTER FIVE
FEAR FACTOR

SARAH TAKES OUT A LARGE TAN ENVELOPE FROM her notebook. Inside are two photographs she printed from websites. She sets the first one on the bench between me and Ava.

"Behold the evidence," she says. "This first photo is from *Horse Behavior*. The article said that in times of crisis, horses and ponies are extremely loyal to their people and stop at nothing to keep them safe. This proves it, I think."

Sarah's right. The photograph shows a pony carrying a young boy across a river to safety. Even though the photo is in black and white, you can tell the river is raging. That boy probably wouldn't have made it across without the pony's help. You can tell the pony is scared, too. Her eyes are wide, and the boy is grabbing her neck.

"They're the bravest of the brave," Sarah says softly. "And *this* one is from *Mane Event*, that site for unicorns and flying horses."

She sets the second photo down. It's a very different story. A single crumpled-up, dirty gym sock is lying on the floor, and a unicorn is standing on his two hind legs, shielding his eyes from the horror like a vampire in sunlight.

"I can top that. Here's more proof unicorns aren't brave," Ava says. "Tiffany Walters was talking about her unicorn at STEAM Team Club last week, and get this — they go out for a walk in the woods the other day, and they hear this noise that sounds like *hoo-hooooo-hoo-hoo, hoo-hooooo-hoo-hoo.*"

"Barred owl," I say.

"Not according to Lemon Drop," Ava says. "That's her unicorn's name. Lemon Drop. Ugh. Anyway, Tiffany said Lemon Drop stopped dead in his tracks and whispered, 'It's the trees. I think they're talking to us.'" Ava snorts and continues. "Tiffany said they heard the noise again. And what did Lemon Drop do? He ran off. Didn't stick around to make sure Tiffany was okay or to find out it was just an owl. Really brave."

"Poor Lemon Drop," Sarah says.

"*Poor Lemon Drop?*" Ava says in disbelief. "Poor Tiffany is more like it."

"Hear me out," Sarah pleads. "Everybody gets scared sometimes. Maybe that's what happened to Lemon Drop. Take Julian, for example. He's *really* afraid of lightning. Aren't you, Julian?"

Enough with the lightning already. How many times do they have to bring that up? I change the subject. "So we have a lot of evidence that unicorns aren't what people think they are. Journals, magazines, websites—"

"But if we're going to be fair, we need *primary* sources," Sarah cuts in, "first-person accounts."

"In other words, we need interviews." I grin. That means getting straight to the heart of the story, just like a real journalist. "And I know who we should interview first." Sarah and Ava look at me with raised eyebrows. "Toby!"

CHAPTER SIX

HOLD YOUR HORSES, ER ... PONIES!

WHEN WE ARRIVE AT THE HENDERSONS' THE NEXT day, the stable is bright white and glowing in the sun. The prancing pony weather vane on the roof turns with a squeak whenever the wind blows.

"Wow!" Ava gasps as it comes into view. "That has to be big enough to hold at least twenty ponies."

"Or unicorns," Sarah adds. Ava glances at me and rolls her eyes.

Most of the animals at the stable are Dr. Henderson's patients, but sometimes, he lets riders keep their horses or ponies here if they don't have a lot of space at home. I guess unicorns are welcome now, too.

Our feet kick up little clouds of gray dust as we walk down the gravel path that leads across the field next to Brandon's house and to the stable.

Ava reaches up and holds her nose. "What *is* that?"

"I was just about to ask the same thing," Sarah says, holding her nose, too.

"Does it smell like crushed dreams and lost hope?" I ask with a smirk.

"More like butterscotch pudding gone bad," Ava says.

"Ah. That would be Sugar," I say.

Sarah stops walking and takes out her notebook. "Observations: rotten pudding smell," she says out loud as she's writing. "Harp music and pink glow coming from far end of stable."

A few oats drift from the giant wooden salad bowl Ava is holding. While we're waiting on Sarah, I look around. The pasture behind the stable is bigger than I remember, and it stretches out until it turns into woods. At the far end, almost where the trees begin, four unicorns are standing so far away I almost mistake them for ponies, until I notice their glowing manes. A fly buzzes around Ava's oats until Sarah snaps her notebook shut, and it flies off.

"So where's Toby?" Sarah asks.

"Follow me," I say, waving toward the stable.

It takes all three of us to open the wooden door. We grab hold of the metal handle. "On the count of three," I say. It's bigger than a garage door, and we all grunt as we slide it open.

Stable smell hits our noses full force, and let me tell you, there's a good reason you don't see barn-scented air fresheners. Since I've been here a lot with Brandon, I know Toby's stall is the last one on the left. Sugar's stall is the last one on the right, as far away from each other as they can get.

I look at the banner that's been hanging in Toby's stall for as long as I can remember, BIRTHDAY PARTY PONY OF THE YEAR. It's so faded you can barely read it.

"Poor Toby," I whisper.

He has his back end facing us, but when he hears my voice, he turns around.

"Oh, it's you, kid. You're late," Toby says with an impatient swish of his tail.

"Sorry," Ava says. "I was looking all over the school for my camera before I realized I left it at home this morning. We brought you some oats!"

Ava holds her mom's salad bowl out, and Toby starts slobbering. Note to self—never eat salad at Ava's again.

"You know what Miss Fancy Pants unicorn gets to eat?" Toby asks between chomps. "Cotton candy."

Ava scrunches her forehead. It's her go-to "I don't believe you" face. I know it well. "That can't be right," she says. "Our science textbook specifically says you have to eat protein and vegetables if you want strong teeth and shiny hair."

Toby snorts, and an oat flies out of his left nostril. Glad I dodged that one.

"That's because we're not magical, sister," he says. "But Corny over there eats flavored air and still looks like a walking rainbow. I'm gray with tan spots on my butt. That's as magical as I get."

"Speaking of magical," I say, "do you and Sugar talk much?"

"Are you kidding?" Toby says, flicking his tail; Ava's fly followed us inside and it's buzzing around his backside. "There's no time for chitchat with unicorns. Always too busy curling their manes or fluffing their tails or some other nonsense." He dips into the oat bowl again. "Hey, kid," he says to Ava. "These are a little stale."

"We only use them to bake oatmeal cookies," Ava says. "The rest of the time they just sit there."

Toby's ears perk up. "You didn't bring any cookies, did you?" Ava shakes her head no. "Too bad," he says, looking truly disappointed.

"Let's get back to the question," I say.

"Hold your horses, kid. I'm getting to it. Where was I? Oh, right. Corn Chowder and her manners. You know, her first day here, I went down to welcome her to the stable—*my* stable. I brought her an apple. You know what she did?"

Sarah is writing as fast as she can. "Tell us," she

says, her eyes never leaving her notebook.

"She takes one look at that apple and says, 'Oh, that's one of those things you Ordinaries eat. No, thank you.' It was a Red Delicious, by the way, not one of those sour Granny Smiths the feed store always has on sale."

Ava looks like she's about to cry, "You poor thing."

"Unicorns have no manners." He shakes his head and a flying piece of oat slobber lands right in the middle of Sarah's forehead.

"So they really are as vain as people say?" Ava asks.

"Wait," Sarah says, wiping away the stale-oat blob with the back of her hand. She's getting frustrated. I know because she's doing that rapid-fire, pencil-tapping thing she does on her notebook. "We shouldn't be asking leading questions. You know, questions you only ask when you want someone to agree with you."

Toby looks at Ava. "Let me ask you this, do you have posters of yourself hanging in your bedroom?"

Sarah laughs.

"It's no joke, Buttercup. They blew up three of her shampoo ads to poster size. One for each wall of her stall."

Sarah's tapping her pencil again. "My name's not Butt—" Toby cuts her off.

"And the mirrors," he says. "This stable didn't have a single one until Unibrow moved in. And that horn. Don't get me started on unicorn horns! Why anyone thinks it's a good idea to keep something around with a spear coming out its forehead is beyond me. Someone's going to lose an eye."

Sarah's tapping so fast I'm waiting for smoke to come from her pencil.

"So how do you feel when Brandon spends so much time with Sugar?" I ask, changing the subject so Sarah doesn't burn a hole in her notebook.

Toby gets quiet and still. He doesn't even try to get rid of the fly that's landed right between his eyes. He drops his head, and his voice is so soft we have to lean in to hear.

"It really hurts," he says. The way he's looking down at his hooves, totally defeated, makes me hurt for him. "Brandon is my kid, you know? And no pony worth his salt takes that lightly. All those pony rides at his birthday parties and sleigh rides in the winter. Walks in the woods. Gone. All that stuff belongs to Corn Chips now."

Toby goes to take another gulp of stale oats but the bowl is empty, and I feel even worse for him. "Brandon came to the stable yesterday after school. Did he come to see me? No. Heads straight for *that one's* stall." He tilts his head toward the other end of the stable. "I had to listen while she sang those annoying unicorn songs to him. Do you know how awful that is? I have hooves; I can't plug my ears."

"That's rough," I say, feeling his pain, and I keep it in mind for the blog.

"It's a lot worse than we thought," Ava says, and turns to me. "When you post about this on *Creature Feature* make sure you write that people have to keep loving ponies more than unicorns—no matter what. You can't stop loving an old thing just because some new, cool thing comes along."

"So you think unicorns are cool?" Sarah asks

Ava, raising her eyebrows.

Toby neighs, "Watch who you're calling old, sister."

"You know," Sarah says, "since we're all here, we should talk to Sugar, too."

What's the point? I think. This is proof that unicorns aren't magic at all; they're self-centered and rude.

Sarah's staring at me and tapping her pencil again.

"Well," I say, "Toby probably has a lot more to tell us, and he deserves some time."

"Yeah," Ava adds. "Especially since he hasn't had much of Brandon's lately."

Sarah folds her arms and looks at the ceiling. Ava and I turn back to Toby.

"So let's talk about what's special about ponies for a while," I say.

For the next twenty minutes Ava and I interview Toby, but Sarah's not making a sound. I turn around to ask her if she has any questions for him, but there's no one to ask.

Sarah's gone.

CHAPTER SEVEN
A HAIR-RAISING CONVERSATION

"SARAH?" I SAY, STILL LOOKING AT THE EMPTY STALL doorway.

"You looking for Notebook Nancy?" Toby asks. "She wandered off fifteen minutes ago. Probably talking to Candy Corn."

I peek around the door of Toby's stall and call out again, louder this time.

"Sarah?!"

My voice echoes down the aisle of the stable. The harp music coming from Sugar's stall seems louder and the pink glow is brighter. I hear sounds in the distance I've never heard before; it's like someone sucked all the helium from a balloon and started singing opera. It stops. Then I see Sarah.

She's waving, walking backward out of Sugar's stall. "Thanks! See you!" she says. "I'm coming!"

she keeps saying as she jogs down the aisle of the stable until she's back at Toby's stall.

"Was I right?" Toby asks. "Were you down there talking to Corn on the Cob?"

"Her name is Sugar, and by the way, my name is Sarah. Not Buttercup. We clear?"

Toby gives a loud neigh and rears slightly, lifting his front legs off the ground. "Yes, ma'am!"

Sarah turns to me and Ava. "And the two of you should talk to Sugar, too—"

Ava cuts her off. "Not this again. We've heard plenty from Toby that proves our point. Poor ponies have been left out in the cold while unicorns claim all the glory."

"Yeah," I say. "After hearing Toby's story, I agree with Ava. What else can Sugar tell us that we don't already know? Besides, we can't do it tonight anyway. It's six o'clock. Dinnertime."

"My favorite time of day!" Toby says as he turns to Ava. "Thanks for the hors d'oeuvre, kid, even if the oats were a little chewy."

Ava picks up her mom's salad bowl that's now

covered in pony slobber, and the three of us leave the stable and head back down the gravel path away from Brandon's. Sarah doesn't waste any time. She opens her notebook and dives in to all things Sugar.

"Okay, so this is the greatest thing ever! Are you ready? Sugar is friends with the Loch Ness Monster. Personal friends. They have each other's numbers and everything. I know because Nessy texted while I was talking to her. Can you believe that?!"

"Wow," I say, flatly.

Ava stops. "No, actually, I can't believe that. Want to know why?"

"I have a feeling you're going to tell me," Sarah says under her breath.

"Because the Loch Ness Monster doesn't exist! Dinosaurs became extinct during the Cretaceous period. You know how long ago that was? Sixty-six million years ago. That's science! You think Sugar has a sixty-six-million-year-old

Plesiosaurus friend who owns a smartphone? Not likely."

We all start walking again, but Ava's not done. "Besides, even if the Loch Ness Monster does exist— which she doesn't—there's no way she can text. She has flippers!"

"Where's your imagination?" Sarah asks.

"Science uses imagination. Lots of imagination. Experiments. Ideas. What it doesn't use is a bunch of made-up fairy tale hooey."

We walk along in silence for a while until Sarah stops. "Okay, so you're not open-minded enough to believe Sugar knows the Loch Ness Monster, but the two of you thinking she's entirely self-centered isn't right, either," she says. "Do you know she gives a strand of her mane to every child she meets, because you're guaranteed happy dreams if you sleep with a unicorn hair under your pillow?"

"Oh, that's even better than a tech-savvy dinosaur!" Ava says.

"I'm serious," Sarah says. "It's such a kind thing to do. Someone vain wouldn't give their hair away to make someone else feel better."

"Yeah, but how do you know she really does? Could just be a good story," I say.

"A good story is exactly what it is," Ava says. "It's a proven fact that good dreams happen when you eat a healthy diet and have enough sleep, not because you have some silly piece of hair under your pillow. Science wins again."

"Not everything can be explained with science," Sarah says. "Some things can only be explained in the heart. Sometimes you have to believe."

"Oh, I believe," Ava says. "I believe in science!"

For some reason, our walk home feels twice as long as usual.

"I saved the best for last," Sarah says. "You know all that harp music and that pink glow?"

"I'm afraid to ask," I say, but I can't help myself. "Yeah?"

Sarah grins. "Unicorn farts," she says. "Sugar's farts sound like someone strumming a harp and they're followed by that pink glow. Isn't that great?!"

"That explains a lot," I say, remembering what

Toby said about her diet.

Ava groans, sounding like a moose with sinus problems. "Okay, that's it. I can't take it anymore. Farts happen because bacteria and gas build up after we eat. You know what that is? Anyone? Anyone?" Ava doesn't wait; she answers her own question. "That's right! It's science! Ava Chen, come on down! You just won *Is It Science or Is It Bogus Unicorn Stories?* Your prize—a brand-new smartphone. It doesn't come with a texting dinosaur, though, because they're all extinct."

I laugh and kick a pebble on the sidewalk. Sarah gets really quiet. I can tell when she's thinking hard about something because she bites her bottom lip. All of a sudden she grins.

"The two of you are right," she says. "I don't know what I was thinking. We have all the information we need from Toby to prove magical creatures aren't all they're cracked up to be."

"I'm glad you've come to your senses," Ava says with a sigh of relief. "You had me worried there for a minute."

"Besides, I'm not sure the two of you could handle talking to Sugar," Sarah says. "In fact, I would strongly advise against it. I would stay as far away from Sugar as possible."

"Why?" Ava asks, narrowing her eyes.

"Because Sugar is one hundred times worse than Toby says she is. In fact, she has to be the most self-centered, vain, thoughtless, smelly, rude unicorn there is. You would not believe her awfulness! I don't think you could handle it," Sarah says.

"Oh, we can handle it." Ava turns to me. "Right, Julian?"

"Right," I say, which is true. If I can handle sharing a bathroom with my brother, I can handle anything.

Sarah shakes her head, "I don't know . . ."

"It's settled. Meet at the lockers tomorrow right after school. Have your questions ready," I say.

Ava nods. "Right. But I'm not bringing that unicorn any cotton candy."

"Based on the amount of harp music we heard today, *no one* should bring her cotton candy," I say as we reach Ava's house.

From her front porch she calls out, "I'll make sure I have my camera tomorrow! Sorry I forgot it!"

"Not as sorry as your mom's going to be when she sees her salad bowl!" I yell over my shoulder as Sarah and I head down the sidewalk toward our houses.

CHAPTER EIGHT
MR. SUNSHINE AND RAINBOW CLOUD

WE MEET AT 3 O'CLOCK THE NEXT DAY BY AVA'S locker. She doesn't have a bowl of oats this time, but she does have her camera.

"You're sure Brandon doesn't mind us coming back today?" Sarah asks.

"I talked to him at lunch," I say. "He said he wants to set the record straight."

When we get to Brandon's, he's sitting at the picnic table next to the white wooden fence by the stable. He waves us over. A tray with chocolate chip cookies sits in the middle of the table.

"My mom says it's rude not to offer guests a snack," he says. "Sugar will be here soon."

I'm reaching for my first cookie when Ava dives right in with the questions. No small talk.

"So, Brandon," she begins. "You mind if I take

some photos for our blog?" She doesn't wait for him to answer before she lifts her camera and snaps a couple shots. "What's so special about that unicorn anyway?"

"What's *not* special about Sugar?" he asks.

"Even better question! That list has to be pretty long," Ava says.

"You know she has the power to give kids good dreams, right?" he says. "And if you touch her horn, it automatically turns sad thoughts into happy ones."

I didn't know about that.

"It's great when I've had a bad day at school or a hard time with a friend . . ." He stops talking and looks away.

"Okay, so back to the horn of destiny," Ava says impatiently. "How does it work exactly?"

"What do you mean?" Brandon asks.

"When you touch the horn, do vibrations activate chemicals in our brains that make us happier?" Ava asks.

"Uh . . ." Brandon looks at Ava like she asked her question in Latin. "No. It just makes you happy. It's magic, I guess."

"But that's impossible, it—" Ava starts, but Sarah cuts her off. "We're gathering information, remember. Not trying to prove points."

"Next question," I say. "How can you ignore poor, old Toby like that? You've had him your whole life."

Brandon looks hurt. "I try not to. It's hard, though. Toby hates Sugar, so I can't spend time with the two of them together. It's one or the other."

"Seems like it's always Sugar," I snap.

Brandon clasps and unclasps his hands, and I see Sarah making a note of it out of the corner of my eye.

"Why does Toby hate Sugar?" I ask.

Brandon starts pumping his knee up and down, making the picnic table shake. He used to do the same thing during soccer games when we were sitting on the bench. Nerves.

"It's my fault," he says quietly. "It's all my fault. My dad told me to have a talk with Toby before we brought Sugar home, but I didn't think it was important. I figured, who doesn't love a unicorn? I didn't think Toby would have any problems. And unicorns are shy. A lot of people don't know that."

"I didn't know that," Sarah says.

"Are you sure?" Ava asks as she snaps another photo. "I haven't come across that in any of my research. Sounds like something unicorns say to excuse bad behavior."

"No, they really are," Brandon says. "It took Sugar three whole days before she felt comfortable enough to talk to me, so when I put her in the stable with Toby, she wouldn't talk to him, either. When she finally did, it was a disaster."

"The apple incident?" I ask.

Brandon nods. "It's been horrible ever since."

"That still doesn't explain why you ignore your pony in favor of a Magical Creature," Ava says.

"Toby's so mad at me I don't want to bother him. Every time I come to the stable, he turns his back, and Sugar's always happy to see me."

"I'd turn my back, too," Ava says.

"Ava," Sarah says, under her breath.

"Well, I would," Ava says. "I'm just being honest."

Brandon is quiet for a minute.

"Sugar is so funny," he finally says. "You should hear her impression of Mrs. Frisner." Brandon lowers his voice and says, "Boys and girls. Boys and girls! If you don't finish your worksheets, there will be no recess!"

I start to laugh, and Ava kicks me under the table.

"She sings lullabies to me while I brush her, too," Brandon says.

"What's so magical about that?" Ava asks. "Toby has great qualities, too. You can't forget about those. He's hardworking, dependable, and sturdy—kind of like a good backpack."

"Like a good *backpack*?" I say to Ava.

"Maybe that's not the best comparison, but Toby deserves some props," she says.

"He's the closest thing I have to a brother. I've known him my whole life," Brandon says. "I know Toby needs me, too. It's just that he's not as . . ." Brandon looks like he's trying to find the right words. "He's not as . . ."

"High maintenance?" Ava suggests. "While we're

on the subject, Sugar is awfully vain. All the posters and the mirrors and the fancy hairdos."

"She wants to be the best unicorn she can be," Brandon says. "Unicorns have a reputation to keep. I get that. She's not perfect, but Toby isn't, either."

"How so?" Sarah asks.

"For one thing, he's grumpy—a lot. Always has been," says Brandon. "Catch him on a bad day, and you'll get an earful about how hard his life is."

I've known Toby as long as I've known Brandon, and it's true. I think back on our conversation with him yesterday. He wasn't exactly Mr. Sunshine.

"He doesn't like to share," Brandon says. "And he's not the easiest to ride. When I'm riding him, I can't tell you the number of times he stops to munch on the taller grass on the other side of the fence. Sometimes he leans over and reaches so far I fall off. He usually doesn't notice. Riding a unicorn is a lot different. Sugar always makes sure I'm safe."

"Huh. Anything else you'd like to add?" I ask.

"Well, you know how Sugar's toots sound like harp music?" Brandon asks, and we all nod. "Toby's definitely DO NOT."

"That's not his fault," Ava says. "It's probably what you feed him. If Toby eats hay and Sugar eats rainbow-colored air, there's bound to be a difference."

As Brandon is telling us about Sugar's diet, something in the distance catches my eye. "She doesn't eat air, but sometimes for a special treat I give her Rainbow Clouds cereal," he says.

"Speaking of rainbow clouds," Sarah says, and points. A yellow, blue, purple, pink blur is moving our way.

"What is that?" Ava asks, and we all watch the blur get closer and closer and closer.

CHAPTER NINE

ORANGE YOU GLAD YOU'RE A UNICORN?

THE RAINBOW BLUR PRANCES UP TO THE FOUR OF us. Sugar. Before she says anything, she raises her right front hoof and she and Brandon exchange their own greeting. It's a kind of fist/hoof bump, and then she lowers her head while he scratches between her ears.

Sugar is a picture-perfect unicorn, and Ava doesn't miss a beat. She lifts her camera and clicks away. She's pearly white all over except for her mane and tail, which glow with strands of every color imaginable. There are glittery orange and pink silk daisies woven all the way down her braided mane. When the sun peeks out from behind a grayish cloud and a beam of light lands on her, the flowers sparkle like diamonds, and so do her hooves.

"So you *do* get your hooves painted all the time?"

Ava asks. "Not just for special stuff, like ads?"

"Oh, yes!" Sugar says. "Who doesn't love a good pedicure?"

Ava gives me one of her sideways glances, then points her camera at one of Sugar's front hooves to get photographic evidence.

"Mrs. Henderson took me to Hair and Hooves Parlor this afternoon. We just got back. They had a new hoof polish—Orange You Glad You're a Unicorn. You like?" she asks Ava, holding out a gleaming tangerine hoof. "It comes in nail polish, too, so you can get some!"

"Oh, good," Ava says sarcastically. "I was hoping."

"It's lovely," Sarah says, elbowing me in the side.

"Uh . . . yeah . . . lovely," I say.

"Did you have a good time?" Brandon asks.

"I suppose, but . . ." Sugar sighs.

"What's wrong?" Brandon asks, worried.

"Well . . . it can be so *hard*," Sugar says. "That's all. People don't realize how difficult it can be. Looking perfect and always being beautiful isn't easy."

"I'll bet," Ava says to me out of the corner of her mouth.

"Today, for example, I had to choose between three new hoof polish colors. Mauve-lous, Orange You Glad You're a Unicorn, and Pixie Party Purple. It took me thirty minutes to decide which one I liked best."

"Thirty minutes," I say. "It takes me less time to do my math homework."

"Maybe that says more about your dedication to your math homework," Sarah says, grinning.

I give her a dirty look, even though she's right.

"I went back and forth. Mauve-lous or Pixie Party? Mauve-lous or Pixie Party? In the end, I went with Orange You Glad You're a Unicorn simply

because I couldn't choose between the other two," Sugar tells us.

"Process of elimination," Sarah says. "That's a math skill, Julian." She's still grinning.

I don't say anything, but the words *stuff it* enter my mind.

"And the silk daisies. Don't get me started," Sugar says.

"We won't!" Ava answers, a little too enthusiastically.

"I mean, hoof color is hard enough, but flower choices are endless!" Without any kind of warning Sugar rears up on her hind legs; her eyes get wide, and one of the silk daisies from her mane flutters to the ground. "Eeeeeek!"

"What's wrong, girl?" Brandon asks.

"Is that a bug? It is. It is a bug. It's a big, ugly, mean bug. Ew! Ew! Ew! Ew! Ew! Make it go away. Make it go away, Brandon!" Now Sugar, still on her hind legs, is backing up so she can get as far away from the big, bad bug as possible, and Ava is snapping shots the whole time.

"It's a ladybug," Sarah says. "It wouldn't hurt . . . well . . . a fly."

"Flies! Where? I don't like them, either," Sugar says.

"No, no," Sarah says. "I just meant . . . never mind."

Brandon plucks a piece of grass and sets it on the ground so the ladybug can climb on board. As he walks away Sugar puts all four hooves back on the ground, and Brandon sets the ladybug down safely on a shrub.

When he sits back down, Ava looks him dead in the eyes. "You have got to be kidding."

"Nobody's perfect," Brandon says. "We're all afraid of something, right? Just ask Julian. He's afraid of lightning."

"Drop it, okay?" I say to Brandon. It comes out louder and angrier than I want it to, but Brandon gets the point. He drops it, but I can tell I hurt his feelings.

For at least twenty seconds nobody says anything, and if you've ever timed it, you know twenty seconds of awkward silence feels more like twenty minutes. I stare at my sneakers until Sugar interrupts.

"It is *such* a beautiful day. Isn't it a *beautiful* day?"

Nobody answers.

"It's the kind of day that's perfect for a walk, which is where I'm headed." Sugar nods her head and we turn to see the four unicorns I saw the other day walking toward us.

"Wow!" Ava says. She seems mesmerized until she catches herself. "Oh, it's only unicorns. I thought it was something special."

"My friends and I were going to stroll in the pasture, but if it's alright with Brandon, it would be more fun to go on the trails in the woods," Sugar says. "Why don't the four of you join us?"

"Uh . . . I don't know . . ." I stall. "It's getting late."

"I've already done all my strolling for the day," Ava mumbles.

"We would LOVE to!" Sarah says, and Sugar flicks her tail in excitement. "Right, Ava and Julian? *Right?*" she says.

"I guess," I say. I don't look over at Brandon to see if he's okay with it. "I'll go, because that's what good journalists do."

"I guess I'll go, too," Ava says. "I can study the other unicorns. For science."

"Goody, goody, goody!" Sugar says.

"Yeah. Goody," Ava says back, without Sugar's enthusiasm.

"This will be a fun ride!" Sugar says.

"Wait. Ride? We're going to *ride* unicorns?" I ask.

Things are going from bad to worse.

CHAPTER TEN
THE REAL MAGIC

"OF COURSE YOU'RE GOING TO RIDE!" Sugar nods.

"I thought unicorns hated giving people rides," Sarah says, folding her arms.

"Silly rumors," the biggest unicorn says as he comes to a stop in front of us. "Where did you get that idea? *Extra-Ordinaries.com*?"

"Maybe," Ava mumbles under her breath.

"We love giving rides," says another unicorn with a high, squeaky voice. "But most people don't know how to ride us properly." My stomach drops. "We're faster than ponies, and if you're not holding on the right way, it's easy to fall off. But don't worry, we'll take it slowly today. We're all in training to work with kids taking unicorn riding lessons. This will be good practice!"

"We don't want anybody getting hurt, so we're selective about whom we let ride," a gray unicorn with a perfectly posh British accent adds.

"That's not on any of the unicorn information pages I've read online," Sarah says.

"You can't believe everything you read just because it's online," the gray unicorn says. "*Anyone* can add *anything* on there, whether it's true or not."

I'm trying to look calm and cool, but inside my stomach is twisting. I've never ridden a unicorn. What if I look stupid? Or fall off?

Sugar looks each of us over from head to toe and then turns to Brandon. "You'll ride Starlight," she says.

"What about you?" Brandon asks Sugar.

"Your mom took me to the salon today to get my mane braided," she says. "I don't want to get it messed up and see all of her money go to waste. I'll be trail guide this time; no rider for me."

Brandon steps up onto a large rock next to the fence by the stable. The boulder seems to be here for this purpose exactly. When standing on it, he's at just the right height to hold onto Starlight's mane and hoist himself onto his back. Starlight is at least a foot taller than Sugar, with a broad chest and muscular legs. He's also neon yellow with a neon-green mane and tail.

Sugar turns to the pale blue unicorn with white stars all over. "Twinkle, why don't you take Sarah."

"Hooray!" Twinkle shouts in her high-pitched voice. She gives a happy whinny as Sarah sits on her back.

I'm next. Sugar looks at me, sizing me up. "Cupcake is the right fit, I think." If Starlight is the biggest unicorn there, Cupcake is the smallest. In human years, she'd be a teenager. She's also light pink with tiny rainbow-colored spots all over, like a confetti cupcake.

I can feel my knees shaking underneath me as I climb onto that rock, but Cupcake gives me a sweet

nuzzle with her nose. Sarah leans over and helps me steady myself on Cupcake's back.

"And last but not least," Sugar says. "Alfred, this is Ava, and she's all yours." When the sun catches the gray unicorn, he turns silver.

"Wait a minute," Ava says, putting her hands on her hips. "What's up with that? The three of them get unicorns that sound like they belong in bakeries or NASA, and I get Alfred?"

"A common misconception," Alfred says with his proper British accent. "We aren't all named after confections and features found in outer space."

"Interesting," Ava says. "Well, you learn something new every day. All right, then, Fred. Let's do this thing." She puts her camera around her neck so she doesn't drop it and steps onto the rock. In a

matter of seconds she's sitting on Alfred's back.

Brandon shows us how to gently grasp some of our unicorn's mane in each hand and wrap it around several times so we can hold on and not fall.

Sugar walks down the row of unicorns and riders like a drill sergeant inspecting her troops, making sure each of us is holding on the right way. Then she makes a series of high-pitched clicking noises, which must mean something in unicorn, and we begin a slow walk across the pasture toward the woods.

As the woods get closer, the unicorns pick up speed, and it feels like we're flying. I've ridden Toby lots of times, and you always feel every lump and bump as you go. Not so with unicorns. Their hooves barely touch the ground; it's like they're gliding, and we cover the pasture in half the time it takes on a pony. I hear myself laugh as the wind rushes through my hair, and I look up at the sky. I don't like what I see.

"Hey, guys!" I shout. "It's going to rain soon. Look."

Nobody cares. Despite the fact she's on a unicorn, Ava has a wicked grin and looks like she's hoping

Alfred outruns the rest of us. She's completely forgotten to take pictures. Sarah is in some sort of dream state; her eyes are closed while she rides. Brandon is deep in conversation with Starlight. I wrap Cupcake's mane around my hands one more time just to be safe.

We reach the edge of the woods, and the sky is even darker now. "Hey, guys!" I yell one more time, but there's still no response. Before I can say anything else we're inside the woods, going deeper and deeper. In fact, we travel so deep in the woods even Brandon doesn't know where we are. Thick, dark moss covers all the rocks and tree trunks. A drop of rain lands right between Cupcake's ears.

"Ahhhh!" she screams, as if it's molten lava instead of water. Another drop hits her rump. "No, no, no!" she says, and starts to rear up.

"It's okay, girl," I say. "It's okay." I stroke her neck, and she puts all four hooves back on the ground, thankfully. The others don't seem to notice until the rain starts getting heavier and heavier.

"We're under attack!" Starlight shouts.

"For heaven's sake. It's just rain!" Ava shouts back.

A bolt of lightning cracks the sky followed by a clap of thunder so loud I feel the ground shake. Cupcake starts twitching and nervously lifting her hooves off the ground. She's settling down again when a second lightning bolt shoots across the sky like a firework. This time, she rears up so fast I let go of her mane, and as she kicks her legs in the air, I slide off her back.

I land on my side and hit the ground so hard it knocks the wind out of me. I see stars. I also see Cupcake running as fast as she can back up the trail, and because unicorns always stick together, the others are following her—except Sugar. Another bolt of lightning fills the sky, and I cover my head with my arms.

"There, there, there." Sugar's voice is soft and low and a little shaky. When I put my arms down, she's standing above me, blocking the rain. I look into her wide, ice-blue eyes, and I can tell she's just as scared as I am. Rain pelts her mane, and most of the silk daisies are hanging by limp strands of drowned unicorn hair. The Orange You Glad You're a Unicorn on her hooves has chipped off, too.

"Are you afraid?" I ask.

"Yes," Sugar answers softly, "more than I've ever been in my life."

"Then why are you still here?" I ask.

"And leave you alone?" Sugar says. "What kind of friend would I be if I did that?"

Lying on the ground in the dark woods, I finally understand why Brandon loves Sugar so much.

Lightning flashes and I cover my head again.

"Julian," she says. "Look at me." I lower my arms. "You're going to be alright. We both are."

"How do you know?" I say.

"I *don't* know for sure," she says. "But I believe we're going to be alright, and believing makes all the difference sometimes." She lowers her head so I can touch her horn. Brandon's right. Happiness rushes through me; it's like waking up and remembering it's your birthday. All the fear of never getting out of the woods goes away; my shoulders relax, then my arms.

"Feeling better?" Sugar asks, and I nod.

I sit up and Sugar lies down beside me to keep me warm. "There's a reason you're so frightened of lightning. What happened? Tell me, please," she whispers.

I look around at the trees that bring back so many memories. "I had a dog," I begin. "Buddy. He was my best friend." I feel like I'm going to cry, but I go on. "We were always together, and one day when I was six years old we wandered off, the two of us."

Sugar nods. "Go on."

"We wandered into the woods behind my house," I said. I never thought I'd share this story with anyone, especially a unicorn.

"I remember walking until it got so dark it felt like we were on another planet. That's when the storm came. The rain was so heavy I could hardly see, but Buddy let me hold onto him. The thunder was so loud I started to cry, but Buddy was there."

Sugar closes her eyes like she's picturing everything I'm telling her.

"The rain wasn't the worst thing," say. "This bolt of lightning came out of the sky. It hit a tree that was so close to us. I remember the tree falling, and when it landed, it only missed us by about ten feet. Buddy could have run off, but he didn't. He stayed right there until the lightning stopped. Somehow he led me all the way back home. My mom's never hugged me harder than she did that day."

"Buddy was a special friend," Sugar says.

I nod. "He was a plain, old, ordinary dog, but he was everything."

"That's the secret, isn't it?" Sugar says.

"What?" I ask.

"What's in here." Sugar gently taps my chest where my heart is with her hoof. "That's the real magic."

The rain is stopping; only a drop or two hits us now and then. Sugar stands. Her tail—the one that earned her two shampoo commercials—is limp and stringy. Her mane is plastered to her neck. She bends low enough that she can scoop me up onto her back, and we begin the journey back through the woods.

As she walks, I hold onto her mane and close my eyes. She starts singing in that helium-high warble.

Sprinkles, cupcakes, red hots, too
Unicorns have rainbow poo
Lemon drops and candy sticks
Unis have no fleas or ticks

Toast's bread but jam's not jelly
Our farts are never smelly
Unicorns love root beer floats
Even though we smell like goats

As we walk along, Sugar keeps singing, and I keep thinking, *Note to self—write Sugar a new unicorn lullaby.*

CHAPTER ELEVEN
SWEET DREAMS

THE NEXT THING I KNOW, I'M LYING ON THE BENCH right outside Sugar's stall.

"He's opening his eyes!" Sarah shouts.

"Of course he's opening his eyes," Ava says. "He's wet, not in a coma."

I laugh when I see Toby, Ava, Sarah, and Brandon standing over me. And Sugar, of course.

If you asked me a week ago whether unicorns were truly magical, I would have told you they were rainbow-colored frauds. But not now.

"What happened out there?" Ava asks, her voice softer than usual.

I tell them everything, about Sugar and the lullabies, and what she did to make sure I was safe. I even tell them why I'm so scared of lightning.

"Wow," Ava says, looking at Sugar, and I'm surprised to hear respect in her voice. She's quiet for a minute, and I can tell she's putting things together in her mind. "So these lullabies . . . Can you explain the theory behind what makes them so effective? Is it chemical? Is it based on sound waves?"

"Sugar," Sarah says, changing the subject, "you're a hero."

Sugar shakes her head. "I did what any good unicorn would do."

"I'm so lucky to have such a great friend," Brandon says to Sugar as he's drying her mane with the blue towel that hangs on the stable wall.

Toby's head droops. "Hooray for unicorns," he says flatly. "Unicorns are special. Unicorns are great. Well, back to the old hole in the wall," and he turns to leave.

"Tobias, wait!" Sugar calls after him. "I have to know! How do you keep your tail so shiny?"

Toby stops and glances over his shoulder. "Wh-what did you say?"

"How do you keep your tail so shiny?" Sugar asks. "I wish mine were as thick and shiny as yours. What's your secret?"

"Uh . . . I eat a lot of grains and hay. A few stale oats . . ." he says, and chuckles to himself.

"Fiber!" Ava says. "That's the most sensible thing I've heard all day."

"You know, they could do amazing things at Hair and Hooves Parlor with that tail," Sugar says, and gives Brandon a nudge, but he's slow on the uptake. *"DON'T YOU THINK THEY COULD DO AMAZING THINGS FOR TOBY AT HAIR AND HOOVES PARLOR, BRANDON?"* She nudges him again.

"Oh! Yeah! I'll ask Mom to make an appointment," Brandon says, hanging the towel back on the wall. He turns and looks at me and Toby. "You know, I'm really lucky to have *three* good friends."

Toby stands a little taller and gives his tail a good swish. "Well, you know, I'm pretty busy, but I'll try to squeeze the parlor in," he says.

I'm the last to walk away from Sugar's stall when she calls me back. I know why, too. She lowers her head so I can reach her mane and pluck a strand of hair.

"Oh, no. That's okay . . ." I say.

"Julian," she says again. This time her voice is firm.

"Which one?" I ask.

"That's a decision only you can make, but you'll know when it's the right one. You'll feel it."

Thousands of glittery strands in every color of the rainbow are in front of me, so I close my eyes and run my fingers through Sugar's mane. A warm, knowing feeling washes over me, and I pluck a single strand from her mane. When I open my eyes, I'm holding a glittering purple lock of unicorn hair. It's glowing and reflects off my white T-shirt and sneakers.

"Keep that under your pillow," she says, "especially during storms."

"C'mon, Julian!" Ava yells from outside the stable. "We're busy people. We all have lives!"

I look into Sugar's clear, blue eyes and wind the unicorn hair around my left pinky, then slip it off my finger and tuck it deep into the front pocket of my jeans.

I start to leave but turn and face Sugar again.

"Thank you," I say. She nods and her mane seems to glow even brighter.

I run to catch up with Ava and Sarah, who are already halfway down the gravel path. I feel the silky strand of Sugar's mane in my pocket, take it out, and look at it again.

"Hey, watcha got there?" Sarah asks.

"Nothing," I say, shoving the unicorn hair back in my pocket.

"Nothing doesn't give off a purple glow," Ava says. "She gave you a strand of hair, didn't she? Wants you to put it under your pillow, doesn't she?"

"Maybe," I say, and shrug.

"But you're not going to, because that's magical nonsense, and unicorn hair has nothing to do with *good* dreams or *bad* dreams or *no* dreams, right?"

I kick a small pebble and it skips along the path.

"A good journalist would try it," I say. "Strictly for investigative purposes, of course."

Sarah agrees with me, and Ava gives us a sideways glance.

"So, in summing up our investigation," I say,

"unicorns aren't as bad as we thought. They do have *some* magical qualities."

Even Ava agrees with me a little bit. "But that doesn't mean *all* magical creatures do," she says. "I bet most of them are downright boring. Take mermaids. What's so magical about them? They can swim. Oooooo."

"I don't know," Sarah says. "Based on Sugar's texts, the Loch Ness Monster is definitely *not* boring."

While Ava and Sarah go back and forth on whether there are dinosaurs still roaming the earth, I take the unicorn hair out of my pocket again. I'm still not completely sure if all unicorns are special, but I know Sugar is.

But the Loch Ness Monster? Mermaids? Those are entirely different stories.